Mitchell Goes Bowling

Hallie Durand

illustrated by Tony Fucile

CANDLEWICK PRESS

Mitchell ALWAYS knocked things down.
That's just how he rolled.

He even tried to knock down his dad. . . .

SLAM!

But one Saturday,

when Mitchell was doing his thing,
his dad caught him and put him
in the car.

Mitchell didn't know where they were going,
but when they got there, he felt right at home.

There were lots of brightly colored balls, a good pizza smell,

and giant crashing noises.

Mitchell got special shoes, too.

"Lane four," the man said.

"That's how old I am!" said Mitchell.

Then he got to type in his name.

Mitchell picked the biggest ball.

He threw it.

"That's called the gutter," his dad said.
Mitchell didn't like the gutter.

He was curious about where his ball had gone . . .

until it popped right out at him!

"You get to go again," said his dad.

Mitchell rolled and knocked two down.

"Battle on!" said Mitchell. He just knew he was going to win.

Then it was his father's turn. He backed all the way up,

swooshed toward the line,

and did a little kick with his leg.

"STRIKE!" said his dad. All the pins had gone down, and his dad got an X.

"Oh," said Mitchell.

On Mitchell's second turn, he did the leg kick, too. But the ball only went a little, so Mitchell ran after it.

The lane was slippery.

That's when the people next door asked for a new lane.

It was his turn again, and Mitchell got a whole side down.
He did a *double* steamin'-hot-potato dance.

Then he knocked another pin down.

But he was pretty sure he was still losing.

Mitchell's dad put his hands over the blowing machine.
He rolled and got another X.

So on Mitchell's turn,

he dried his hands,

his face,

and his hair,

then stuck his fingers in the holes and did the leg kick.

He only knocked three down.

"FINE," said Mitchell. He really, really wanted an X.

He didn't get any on the next few frames.

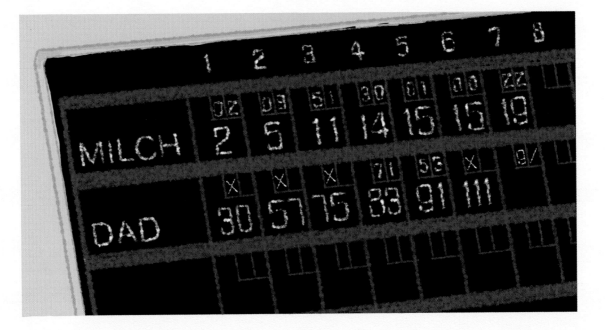

Mitchell really wanted to win, so when he picked
up his next ball, he yelled . . .

He THREW. . . .

He prayed. . . .

NOTHING.

"I'M GOING HOME," Mitchell said.

And that's when Mitchell's dad said,
"Hey, want to be on the same team?"

Mitchell thought
for a second.

With his dad,
he couldn't lose.

He wanted an X.
He wanted to win.

"Deal," said Mitchell.

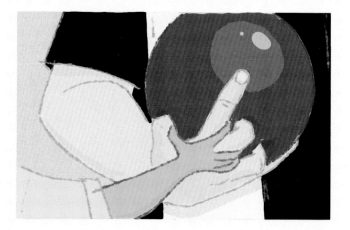

Mitchell and his dad
dried their hands,

picked up the ball,

swung their arms all the way back,

and they did a little kick.

Shhheeeeeeeeeeeeeeeeeeeeeeeee—PLUNK!

That ball went sailing right down the middle and . . .

SSSSSSSSSSSSSSSSSSSSSSSSTTTTTTTTRRRR

RRRRRRIIIIIIIIIIIKKKKKKKKKKKKE!

They did a triple steamin'-hot-potato dance, *with salsa*!

Then Mitchell looked his dad right
in the eyeballs and said,

"Battle on!"

And that's just what they did.

For Tony Fucile, XXX
H. D.

To Eli and Elinor
T. F.

Big thanks to my friends Antonio and Larry at Hanover Lanes in East Hanover, NJ.
H. D.

Text copyright © 2013 by Hallie Durand
Illustrations copyright © 2013 by Tony Fucile

First edition 2013

Library of Congress Catalog Card Number 2012947730
ISBN 978-0-7636-6049-9

13 14 15 16 17 18 TLF 10 9 8 7 6 5 4 3 2 1

Printed in Dongguan, Guangdong, China

This book was typeset in Shannon.
The illustrations were done digitally.

Candlewick Press
99 Dover Street
Somerville, Massachusetts 02144

visit us at www.candlewick.com